Best Birthday Ever!

Written by Peter Bently

Illustrated by Steve May

One day, Ana woke up feeling very excited because it was her birthday.

After breakfast, she opened all her presents. She was delighted with the one from Mum and Dad, which was a book about snakes.

"Great!" she declared. "Snakes are my favourite animals!"

Arun gave her a toy snake.

"Wow, brilliant!" gasped Ana. "It looks so real!"

Arun helped Mum to make the birthday picnic.

"What's inside that enormous tin?" asked Arun.

"Just wait and see," smiled Mum.

Ana and Dad packed the car, ready to
go to the beach.

"Anything else we need?" asked Dad.

"I'm taking my new snake to play with,"
said Ana.

They arrived and unpacked everything.
Then Mum and Dad sunbathed while Asha
got to work building sandcastles.

Arun wanted to paddle in the sea.
"You coming, Ana?" he called out.

"No thanks," replied Ana. "I'm playing
with my snake. It's a huge cobra. Look out!"

When it was nearly time for lunch, Ana and Arun laid out the food on the rug. Asha was still making sandcastles.

"Asha, be careful not to throw any sand over here," warned Mum. "We don't want to ruin the picnic!"

"That's right," chuckled Arun. "There's nothing worse than sandy sandwiches!"

9

"This picnic looks delicious," said Dad, reaching for a chicken drumstick.

"Wait for Ana," frowned Mum. "It's her birthday, after all."

Ana was wandering up and down, staring at the sand.

"Come on Ana," called Dad. "You don't want to miss your own birthday picnic!"

"I'm looking for my snake," wailed Ana. "It's disappeared!"

They looked everywhere for Ana's snake: under the towels, in the beach bags, even under the picnic rug – but there was no sign of it.

"It might have been washed out to sea!" moaned Ana.

Suddenly Puff started to bark.

"What's the matter with Puff?" said Arun. "It looks like he's found something."

Puff was standing by a rock, barking loudly.

"Oh, well done, Puff!" Arun exclaimed. "Ana, Puff has found your snake!"

He bent down to have a closer look …

then he sprang back in alarm.
"Eek!" he screeched. "It's alive! Help!"

Ana watched the snake slithering away.
"Don't worry," she laughed. "It's only a
slowworm. It's totally harmless!"

"Are you sure that snake wasn't poisonous?" Arun asked, when they were all back sitting on the rug.

"Oh yes," smiled Ana. "It's in my book. In fact, a slowworm isn't a snake. It's a legless lizard."

"Well, I never knew that," said Dad. "How interesting."

The picnic was delicious. Afterwards,
Asha fell asleep under the big beach
umbrella.

"She's tired out from building such
a giant sandcastle!" laughed Mum.

Arun and Ana started a game of
football. Puff joined in too.
"I'm really enjoying my birthday!"
grinned Ana. "Even if I have lost
my snake."

Suddenly, Arun slipped and kicked the
ball the wrong way.

"Look out!" yelled Ana. "It's heading straight for Asha!"

Puff dived for the ball and knocked
it out of the way just in time.

"Good boy, Puff!"
cried Arun. "You
saved Asha!"

The family looked at the heap of sand that had once been Asha's sandcastle.

"It's a total wreck," said Dad. "Let's build it again before Asha wakes up."

Then Arun sprang back in alarm. "Look, another snake!" His voice shook. "This one looks poisonous!"

Ana peered at the snake, and then laughed. "It's my toy snake!" she said. "Asha must have buried it by mistake!" Ana was thrilled to have her snake back.

"And now it's time for Ana's secret surprise," chuckled Mum, opening the enormous tin that Arun had spotted earlier.

Inside was a birthday cake in the shape of a snake.

"This one's definitely not poisonous!" laughed Dad.

"It's brilliant, thank you!" grinned Ana. "This is the best birthday ever!"